KING PIG

For Niah, Elan, Tais and Ezra

First published by Scholastic Australia in 2013

ISBN 978-0-545-67013-5

12 11 10 9 8 7 6 5 4 3 2 1   13 14 15 16 17 18/0

Printed in the U.S.A.   40

This edition first printing, December 2013

Typeset in Lomba

KING PIG

Nick Bland

SCHOLASTIC INC.

King Pig could never understand why the sheep didn't adore him. They were always complaining about one thing or another.

They hardly ever smiled

and when they did, King Pig
thought they were teasing him.

They never listened properly,
no matter how loudly he shouted.

And the harder
he tried to get
their attention . . .

the more they ignored him.

Because he was the king, he could make the sheep
do whatever he wanted . . .

whenever he pleased.

But he just couldn't make them *like* him.

"Maybe they would like me more if I looked . . . fancier," said King Pig. For that, he would need a lot of fancy new clothes.

But who could he get to make them?

King Pig woke up all the sheep
and invited them into his nice,
warm castle.

And there he slept while the sheep went to work.
They gathered up every last snippet of their wool

and they knit, knit, knitted all through the night
until the king had his pile of fancy new clothes.

In the morning, King Pig was ready to prance.
He looked . . .

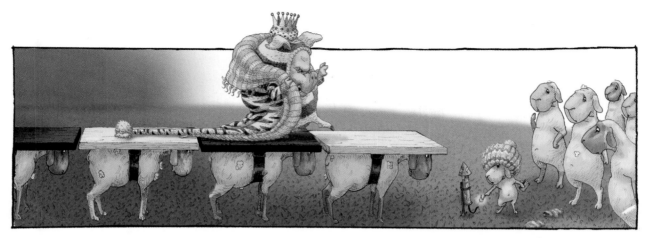

He was ferocious.

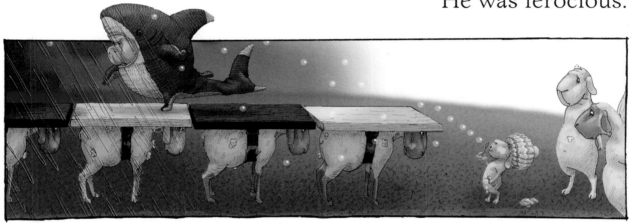

He was fearless.

He was the best-dressed king in the kingdom.

But when he stopped to take a bow, nobody was watching.

Nobody was cheering. Nobody was *adoring* him.

"Maybe you could try being nice," said a little voice.

"But I thought I *was* being nice!" said King Pig,
and he went inside to sulk.